T0353822

YORKIPOO BLUE
AND HER
FIRST DAY OF SCHOOL

A TAIL OF TWO FUR-EVER FRIENDS

KELLY TIREY

This tinder hearted book was inspired by a courageous thought and a loving nudge from God to chase a childhood dream.

This endearing story is dedicated to my inspiring children, my butterfly Delilah, a husband who is forever giving, parents who are unequivocally devoted to my ultimate happiness, friends and family who have never left, my Aunt Shannon who wears her heart on her sleeve and a wonderful mother in law who claims me as her own!

Also, to Pervaiz, a man who loved deeply and provided his family with such joy during his precious time here.

-- Now to my readers: lean in here really closely please! Feel that? It's a huge hug for you!

WELCOME TO THE FAMILY my little Yorkipoo Blue friends. YOU are now a part of this adorable journey, so may your hearts be filled with magic and your smiles shine brighter!

"Love Makes The Sweetest Paw Prints On Our Lives." --

Author

Illustrator

Yorkipoo Blue
and her FIRST
day of school!
A tail of two fur-ever friends.

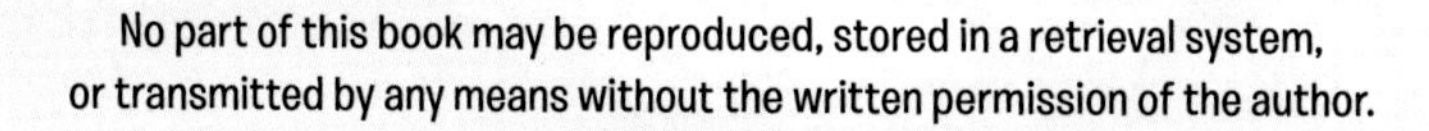

AuthorHouse™
1663 Liberty Drive
Bloomington, IN 47403
www.authorhouse.com
Phone: 833-262-8899

This book is printed on acid-free paper.

ISBN: 979-8-8230-3086-1 (sc)
ISBN: 979-8-8230-3106-6 (hc)
ISBN: 979-8-8230-3087-8 (e)

Library of Congress Control Number: 2024915440

Print information available on the last page.

Published by AuthorHouse 08/13/2024

authorHOUSE®

YORKIPOO BLUE

AND HER FIRST DAY OF SCHOOL

A TAIL OF TWO FUR-EVER FRIENDS

LUV330

KELLY TKREY

Oh my! Pup School is starting in just one week,
excited as can be, Yorkipoo Blue lets out a squeak.

She studies colors, numbers and letters galore,
this jolly Yorkipoo can't wait to learn more.

**Blue brushes her wavy hair, lays out her purple bows,
can't forget to paint those tiny Yorkipoo toes.**

It’s the morning of her very first school day,
Yorkipoo Blue feels nervous and whimpers to stay.

Momma dances around the kitchen making her giggle,
in fact she laughs so hard that she wiggles.

"You must remember you are smart, fun and neat,
think of the different furry friends you'll meet."

Blue begins packing up her 'woofles' extra fast,

as her yellow puppy school bus is here at last!

Blocks, crayons, golden doodle markers and more,
this learning stuff will be better than anything before.

A doggie named Poodle Sue was sitting ever-so shyly,
Blue barked up the courage to help her become smiley.

This bashful fluff ball felt super happy making a friend,
now snickering to herself Poodle Sue is on the mend.

The teacher smiles giving Blue a crunchy reward treat,
“Thank you for being brave, thoughtful and sweet.”

Tick-Tock
Tick-Tock
LUNCH TIME
1+1=2

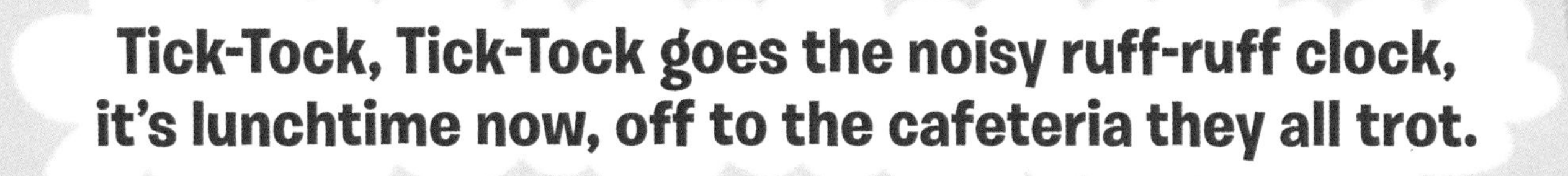
Tick-Tock, Tick-Tock goes the noisy ruff-ruff clock,
it's lunchtime now, off to the cafeteria they all trot.

Popcorn 2.00
Sandwich 6.00
Cake 3.00
Fruit bowl 2.75
Bread 1.00
Salad 5.00
HAHAHAHAHAHH
100%
100%

**Blue and Sue sit down side by side to eat,
telling jokes so silly they can barely stay in their seat.**

"What's a cats favorite sport?"

"What's a cats favorite sport?" Yorkipoo asks them all, before anyone could answer she howls "hairball."

Bellies and brains are now full of exciting fun things,
back to class to wonder what the next day brings.

Each student packs up their doggie-bags and tools,
one should always follow the 'good dog' rules.

Bye...

Snuggles to the teachers, high fives to friends,
Yorkipoo must not forget them as the day ends.

Up go the animal books and off go the class lights,
"I can't wait to see you again," says Mrs. Bright.

OFF
Yorkipoo
6
4
3
5
1

Poodle glances around hoping to catch Yorkipoo's eye,
blushing and gushing the pooches ruff their goodbye.

Having merrily skipped to the buses feeling as if she could fly,
Blue sees the most angelic butterflies sweeping the sky.

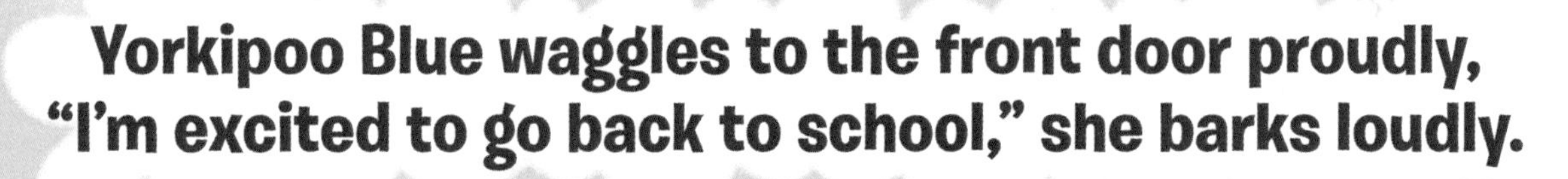

Yorkipoo Blue waggles to the front door proudly,
"I'm excited to go back to school," she barks loudly.

I AM
OF

ROUD

OU

YOU
ARE THE
BEST

Momma and Daddy are giving Blue a new bandanna,
"keep this safe and close it was knitted by your Nana."

Jumping up and down she tells her mom all about Sue,
along with the yummy treats she was given to chew.

SCHOOL

"I worked through my fears with all of my might,
school isn't scary anymore," she says with delight.

Momma smiles a mile wide seeing her pup blossom,
the joy shining on Blue's face is doggone paw-some!

QUESTION CORNER:

Who is your favorite character in this book and why?

Have you been shy before? Can you explain how you worked through it?

- I AM PROUD OF YOU -

Guess what? In the next book we get to learn Momma Blues first name...

HINT it starts with the letter "M."

Printed in the United States
by Baker & Taylor Publisher Services